Jpb   90-01323
ZOL   12.89
   Zolotow, Charlotte

Someday.

Withdrawn

S0-CEY-455

Officially Noted

stain, paper residue on other side. 2/17 DS

SOMEDAY

by Charlotte Zolotow
pictures by Arnold Lobel

Harper & Row, Publishers · New York, Evanston & London

For Ellen right now

SOMEDAY
Text copyright © 1965 by Charlotte Zolotow
Pictures copyright © 1965 by Arnold Lobel
Printed in the United States of America. All rights reserved.

Library of Congress Catalog Card Number: 64-16654

90-01323

SOMEDAY I'm going to go to school

and everyone will say,
"How beautiful you look today. I wish I had hair like yours!"

someday

I'm going to come home
and my brother
will introduce me
to his friends and say,
"This is my sister."
Instead of
"Here's the family creep."

SOMEDAY

I'm going to go to dancing class

and Miss Bird will say,
"Ellen is doing it just right. Everybody watch her."

Someday

I'm going to catch a high, high ball

and my team will win because I did it.

SOMEDAY

I'll have one hundred dollars
and I'll buy presents
for everyone I know,
and when they thank me I'll say,

"Oh, it isn't anything. . . ."

SOMEDAY

I'm going to water my plant

and find it covered with pink flowers the way it was when it first came.

SOMEDAY

my mother and father are going to say,

"Why are you going to bed so early?"

SOMEDAY

I'm going to have a little bulldog
who sleeps on my bed at night

and won't eat unless *I* feed him.

SOMEDAY

when I have nothing to read,
the doorbell will ring

FOR ME

and a big box of books will come for me.

SOMEDAY my mother will say to me,

"Please set the table with all the best china
for dinner tonight.
None of the everyday things."

SOMEDAY

I'm going to be practicing the piano
and the lady across the street
will call and say,

"Please play that
beautiful piece again!"

SOMEDAY

I'm going to walk through this very same house
and find a room I've never found before.

SOMEDAY

I am going to decorate the Christmas tree my own way

without my mother or my father or my brother helping.

But right now . . . it's dinnertime.